The gift you never
knew you wanted.

THIS BOOK IS NOT A PRESENT

WRITTEN BY
MAX GREENFIELD

ILLUSTRATED BY
MIKE LOWERY

putnam

G. P. Putnam's Sons

THIS BOOK IS NOT A PRESENT.

I KNOW IT WAS

DISGUISED

AS A PRESENT,

ALL BEAUTIFULLY

WRAPPED WITH A

BOW AND CARD ATTACHED,

I JUST KEEP RELIVING THE MOMENT IN MY **HEAD**— THE MOMENT JUST BEFORE I UNWRAPPED IT.

EVEN SOCKS WOULD HAVE BEEN A GREAT PRESENT BECAUSE AT LEAST SOCKS WOULD KEEP MY FEET WARM WHILE RIDING MY SKATEBOARD

AND PLAYING WITH WHAT SHOULD HAVE BEEN MY NEW DOG.

I WOULD'VE NAMED THE DOG BINGO.

NOSE ↓

KABOOM ↓ !

FIG. 3A ↑

THIS BOOK IS NOT A PRESENT FOR ONE REASON AND ONE REASON ALONE:

NOW I FEEL LIKE I HAVE TO READ IT.

IF I'M BEING HONEST,
I DIDN'T EVEN REALLY WANT
TO READ THE CARD...

THIS MORNING, FOR INSTANCE, I HAD A **GLORIOUS** TIME MAKING MYSELF A **WAFFLE SANDWICH** FOR **BREAKFAST,**

OR AS I LIKE TO CALL THEM,

WAFFLEWICHES.

I'M YUMMY!

HOWEVER, JUST BECAUSE I LIKE TO COOK DOESN'T MEAN I HAVE ANY INTEREST IN READING A COOKBOOK.

AW!

THE SAME GOES FOR READING ANY KIND OF

INSTRÜCTIONS

① Step One

A BOOK IS NOT A PRESENT.

AW

② Step Two

NEITHER IS A BOOK OF INSTRUCTIONS THAT MIGHT BE INCLUDED WITH A PRESENT, MAKING THAT PRESENT NOT A PRESENT.

GRR

BLAH BLAH

ALSO, AS IF I HAVE TIME TO READ A BOOK. LIKE I SAID, I'M VERY BUSY DOING THINGS. AND WHEN I'M NOT DOING THINGS, I'M THINKING ABOUT THINGS.

I THINK ABOUT THINGS ALL THE TIME, AND MY THOUGHTS ARE GREAT.

BOOKS ARE FULL OF SOMEONE ELSE'S THOUGHTS, AND EVEN THOUGH READING SOMEONE ELSE'S THOUGHTS SOUNDS LIKE A SUPERPOWER,

IT'S NOT ONE I WANT.

HOW LONG IS THIS
BOOK, ANYWAY?

HOW MANY PAGES HAVE
I READ SO FAR?

TWENTY-
TWO?!

AND IT'S NOT
DONE YET???

THIS BETTER NOT BE A CHAPTER BOOK.

IF THIS BOOK IS A CHAPTER BOOK, I'M GOING TO ABSOLUTELY

EXPLODE!

I MEAN, WHAT TYPE OF PERSON GIVES ANOTHER PERSON A CHAPTER BOOK AND CALLS IT A PRESENT!?!

CHAPTER
2
Gratitude

DON'T GET ME WRONG,
I **AM** APPRECIATIVE

(I MEAN, NOT FOR THE THANK-YOU NOTE
THAT I DEFINITELY DON'T WANT TO WRITE).

AND WHEN ASKED, I'LL SAY THAT I'VE READ THIS BOOK. AND THEN...

(JUST LIKE THE TIME MY PARENTS WANTED TO KNOW IF IT WAS ME WHO CLOGGED THE TOILET WITH HOMEMADE SLIME AND I TOLD THEM IT MOST DEFINITELY WASN'T ME EVEN THOUGH THAT SAME SLIME WAS ALL OVER MY SHOES AND TOWELS)

... FOR THE SECOND TIME IN MY LIFE, I WILL BE LYING.

NOW I'M A LIAR, AGAIN.

I CAN'T IMAGINE A SINGLE OCCASION THAT WOULD MAKE IT OKAY TO GIVE SOMEONE A BOOK AS A PRESENT.

NOT CHRISTMAS

NOT FLAG DAY

NOT A BIRTHDAY

NOT TAX DAY

NOT CHANUKAH

NOT KWANZAA

NOT THE
4TH OF JULY

NOT
GROUNDHOG
DAY

NOT
VALENTINE'S
DAY

NOT
EASTER

NOT NATIONAL
DOUGHNUT DAY

NOT
EVEN CINCO
DE MAYO

DEFINITELY NOT
HALLOWEEN

MAYBE
APRIL FOOLS' DAY

I WOULD NEVER DO THIS TO SOMEONE.

WHY?

BECAUSE I'M AN INCREDIBLE LISTENER, AND I'VE (NEVER) HEARD (ANYONE) SAY THAT THEY WANT A BOOK AS A PRESENT.

> IF A TREE FALLS IN THE WOODS DOES IT MAKE A SOUND?

THE ANSWER IS **YES.**
I HEARD THE TREE BECAUSE THAT'S HOW GOOD A LISTENER I AM, AND IT SAID ⟶

PLEASE DON'T TURN ME INTO A BOOK.

I WISH SOMEONE WOULD HAVE LISTENED TO ME. MAYBE THEN THEY WOULD HAVE TURNED THE TREE INTO AN

ELECTRIC GUITAR

THANK GOODNESS—IT LOOKS
LIKE I'M DONE WITH
THIS BOOK THAT'S
STILL NOT A PRESENT.

AT LEAST NOW
IF SOMEONE
ASKS, I'LL BE ABLE TO SAY THAT

I'VE
READ
IT.

I GUESS THEN I'LL HAVE
ONLY LIED ABOUT THE SLIME.

FINISHING THIS BOOK DOES FEEL LIKE THE PERFECT PRESENT TO MYSELF. MAYBE I'LL WRITE (ME) A THANK-YOU NOTE.

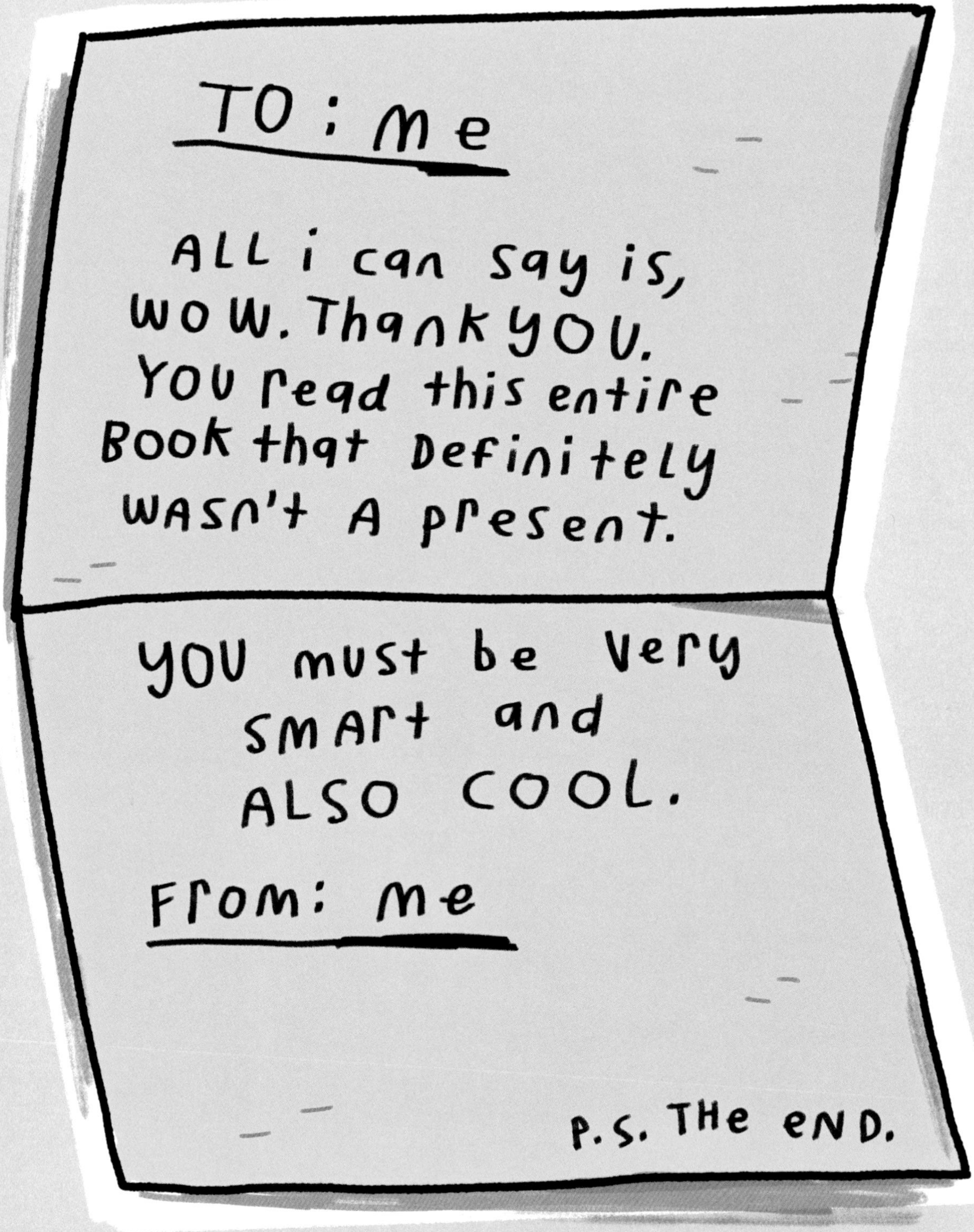
TO: me
ALL i can say is, wow. Thank you. You read this entire Book that Definitely wasn't A present.
You must be very smart and ALSO COOL.
From: me
P.S. THE END.

THERE. MY CONSCIENCE
IS NOW CLEAN.

To my son, Ozzie, one of the best
presents I have ever received.
—M.G.

Dedicated to WC Houston.
—M.L.

G. P. Putnam's Sons
An imprint of Penguin Random House LLC, New York

First published in the United States of America by G. P. Putnam's Sons,
an imprint of Penguin Random House LLC, 2022
Text copyright © 2022 by Max Greenfield
Illustrations copyright © 2022 by Mike Lowery

Visit us online at penguinrandomhouse.com

Library of Congress Cataloging-in-Publication Data is available.

Printed in the United States of America

ISBN 9780593462362

1 3 5 7 9 10 8 6 4 2

PC

Design by Eileen Savage | Text set in Pitch Or Honey Sans
The art was done first with pencils and then with digital media.